For Samuel and Orlando
L.C.

Printed in Hong Kong   First Edition   10 9 8 7 6 5 4 3 2 1

Library of Congress Cataloging in Publication Data
Cecil, Laura.
Boo! : stories to make you jump.
Summary: A collection of scary stories and poems,
with an emphasis on monsters, ghosts, and witches.
1. Supernatural—Literary collections. [1. Supernatural—
Literary collections]   I. Clark, Emma Chichester, ill. II. Title.
PZ5.C27   1990   820.8'037   90-2824   ISBN 0-688-09842-8

BOO!

Stories to Make You Jump

Compiled by Laura Cecil
Illustrated by Emma Chichester Clark

Greenwillow Books, New York

ACKNOWLEDGMENTS

Thanks are due to the following for permission to reprint copyright material:
'Countdown' from *It's Halloween* by Jack Prelutsky. Text copyright © 1977 by
Jack Prelutsky. Reprinted by arrangement with Greenwillow Books, a division
of William Morrow and Company, Inc. 'The King o' the Cats' taken from
Joseph Jacobs' *English Fairy Tales* (Bodley Head). 'The Wendigo' from *Verses
from 1929 on* by Ogden Nash. Copyright © 1953 by Ogden Nash. Reprinted
with permission from Little, Brown and Company and Curtis Brown Ltd.
Diana Wynne Jones for 'The Thing' © Diana Wynne Jones 1985. Used by
permission from the author. Robin and Jocelyn Wild for 'Scribbling Tess' ©
Robin and Jocelyn Wild 1984. Used by permission of the authors. 'The Three
Billy-Goats-Gruff' reprinted from Peter Christen Asbjornsen's *Popular Tales
from the Norse,* translated by G. W. Dasent. This retelling © 1990 Laura Cecil.
'Elisabeth the Cow Ghost' reprinted by arrangement with the Watkins/Loomis
Agency Inc. Copyright © 1936, 1963, 1964 by William Pène du Bois.
Originally published by The Viking Press. 'The Catipoce' by permission of the
James Reeves Estate © 1957 James Reeves. 'The Strange Visitor' taken from
Joseph Jacobs' *English Fairy Tales* (Bodley Head). 'The Ghost Who Came out of
the Book' reprinted with permission of Margaret K. McElderry Books, an
imprint of Macmillan Publishing Company, and Dent from *Non-Stop Nonsense*
by Margaret Mahy. Text copyright © 1977 Margaret Mahy. 'The Small
Ghostie' © Barbara Ireson 1984. Used by permission of the author. 'Jackie and
the Ogre' by permission of the James Reeves Estate © James Reeves 1977. 'The
Little Wee Tyke' traditional Northumberland/English from *Forgotten Folktales
of the English Counties* by Ruth L. Tongue © 1970 Ruth L. Tongue by
permission of Routledge.

Every effort has been made to trace all the copyright holders, and the publishers
apologize if any inadvertent omission has been made.

Contents

Countdown 9
Jack Prelutsky

The King o' the Cats 11
Joseph Jacobs

The Wendigo 16
Ogden Nash

The Thing 18
Diana Wynne Jones

Scribbling Tess 24
Robin and Jocelyn Wild

The Three Billy-Goats-Gruff 28
Traditional

The Dark Wood 34
Traditional

Elisabeth the Cow Ghost 36
William Pène du Bois

The Catipoce 47
James Reeves

The Strange Visitor 50
Joseph Jacobs

Old Roger Is Dead and Laid in His Grave 58
Traditional

The Ghost Who Came out of the Book 60
Margaret Mahy

The Hairy Toe 72
Traditional American

The Small Ghostie 76
Barbara Ireson

Jackie and the Ogre 78
James Reeves

Two Witches' Charms 84
Ben Jonson

The Little Wee Tyke 86
Traditional

"From Ghoulies and Ghoosties, Long
Leggety Beasties, And Things That Go
Bump In The Night,
            Good Lord Deliver Us!"

Countdown
Jack Prelutsky

There are ten ghosts in the pantry,
There are nine upon the stairs,
There are eight ghosts in the attic,
There are seven on the chairs,
There are six within the kitchen,
There are five along the hall,
There are four upon the ceiling,
There are three upon the wall,
There are two ghosts on the carpet,
Doing things that ghosts will do,
There is one ghost
   right
     behind me
       Who is oh so quiet . . . . .

The King o' the Cats
Joseph Jacobs

ONE winter's evening the sexton's wife was sitting by the fireside with her big black cat, Old Tom, on the other side, both half asleep and waiting for the master to come home. They waited and they waited, but still he didn't come, till at last he came rushing in, calling out, "Who's Tommy Tildrum?" in such a wild way that both his wife and his cat stared at him to know what was the matter.

"Why, what's the matter?" said his wife. "And why do you want to know who Tommy Tildrum is?"

"Oh, I've had such an adventure. I was digging away at old Mr Fordyce's grave when I suppose I must have dropped asleep, and only woke up by hearing a cat's *Miaou*."

"*Miaou!*" said Old Tom in answer.

"Yes, just like that! So I looked over the edge of the grave, and what do you think I saw?"

"Now, how can I tell?" said the sexton's wife.

"Why, nine black cats all like our friend Tom here, all with a white spot on their chestesses. And what do you think they were carrying? Why, a small coffin covered with a black velvet pall, and on the pall was a small coronet all of gold, and at every third step they took they cried all together, *Miaou—*"

"*Miaou!*" said Old Tom again.

"Yes, just like that!" said the sexton. "And as they came nearer and nearer to me I could see them more distinctly, because their eyes shone out with a sort of green light. Well, they all came toward me, eight of them carrying the coffin, and the biggest cat of all walking in front for all the world like — but look at our Tom, how he's looking at me. You'd think he knew all I was saying."

"Go on, go on," said his wife. "Never mind Old Tom."

"Well, as I was a-saying, they came toward

me slowly and solemnly, and at every third step crying all together, *Miaou*—"

"*Miaou!*" said Old Tom again.

"Yes, just like that, till they came and stood right opposite Mr Fordyce's grave, where I was, when they all stood still and looked straight at me. I did feel queer, that I did! But look at Old Tom; he's looking at me just like they did."

"Go on, go on," said his wife. "Never mind Old Tom."

"Where was I? Oh, they all stood still looking at me, when the one that wasn't carrying the coffin came forward and, staring straight at me, said to me — yes, I tell 'ee, *said* to me, with a squeaky voice, 'Tell Tom Tildrum that Tim Toldrum's dead,' and that's why I asked you if you knew who Tom Tildrum was, for how can I tell Tom Tildrum Tim Toldrum's dead if I don't know who Tom Tildrum is?"

"Look at Old Tom, look at Old Tom!" screamed his wife.

And well he might look, for Tom was swelling and Tom was staring, and at last Tom shrieked out, "What — old Tim dead! Then I'm the King o' the Cats!" and rushed up the chimney and was never more seen.

The Wendigo
Ogden Nash

The Wendigo,
The Wendigo!
Its eyes are ice and indigo!
Its blood is rank and yellowish!
Its voice is hoarse and bellowish!
Its tentacles are slithery,
And scummy,
Slimy,
Leathery!
Its lips are hungry blubbery,
And smacky,
Sucky,

Rubbery!
The Wendigo,
The Wendigo!
I saw it just a friend ago!
Last night it lurked in Canada;
Tonight, on your veranada!
As you are lolling hammockwise,
It contemplates you stomachwise.
You loll,
It contemplates,
It lollops.
The rest is merely gulps
    and gollops.

The Thing
Diana Wynne Jones

Syreta was afraid of the bathroom cupboard. She said there was a Thing in it. Her brother Richard laughed at her and her mum scolded her, but Syreta was sure there was a Thing. Every time she had a bath, she screamed:

"No, no, no! There's a Thing!"

Her mum tried to cure Syreta the same way she cured Richard of stealing biscuits. She was very stern. "There is *no* Thing," she said. "Stop that silly noise!"

But Syreta was still scared and she screamed louder than ever. So Mum took Syreta into the bathroom and made Richard open the cupboard. She and Richard took out all the sheets and the towels and the spare blanket and the old nappies, until the cupboard was empty. "There!" said Mum. "Can you see a Thing in there?"

Syreta sobbed and gulped and stared nervously in at the bare wooden shelves and the pipes at the back. "I don't know," she said. "I don't know what the Thing looks like."

"Perhaps it's invisible," Richard suggested.

"Don't *you* start now!" said Mum. She piled all the things back into the cupboard. Then she tried to cure Syreta by sending her into the bathroom to fetch things. "Syreta, fetch me the little red towel by the wash basin," she said. "Quickly now!"

Syreta was so scared that she went slowly, slowly. She squeezed round the bathroom door and went slowly, slowly round the bathroom with her back to the wall. As soon as her hand was on the towel, she grabbed it and ran away screaming harder than ever.

Richard got annoyed. I'll give her something to be scared about, he thought. So, when Mum sent Syreta to fetch the yellow tooth mug, Richard sneaked into the bathroom first and hid under the sheets in the cupboard. After a bit, he heard the door creak open and then the rubbing sound of Syreta sliding round the room with her back to the wall. He put a sheet over his face and stuck his head out of the cupboard.

"GRAAH!" he roared. "I'm the Thing!"

There was such a dead silence that Richard pulled the sheet up so that he could see Syreta out of one eye. She was standing staring. Her face was such a strange color that Richard was afraid he had killed her.

"I'm not fierce," he said hurriedly. "I don't eat people. I only eat biscuits."

To his surprise, Syreta's chin went up and her face turned the proper color. "I'm not scared," she said. "I know what you look like now. I'll bring you a biscuit every day." And she went skipping away to give Mum the yellow tooth mug.

Syreta never screamed about the Thing again. But now Mum is trying to cure Syreta of hiding biscuits in the bathroom cupboard. Some days, there is a whole pile of biscuits in there. Other days, there are only crumbs. Those days, of course, are when Richard gets to the cupboard before Mum does.

Scribbling Tess
Robin and Jocelyn Wild

They say that when Teresa Mould
Was hardly twenty-four hours old
Her parents found the tiny tot
Scribbling on her carry cot.
At first the Moulds were filled with pride,
"Our child's a genius!" they cried.
But as Teresa Mould grew older
Her busy fingers grew much bolder.
Soon the window sills, the stairs,
The bath, the sofa and the chairs,
And every single inch of wall
Were covered in her childish scrawl.
Mr Mould was in despair.
He said, "We need a change of air.
We'll take our trying little daughter
To stay at Tooting-on-the-Water."
Starting off at nine next day
They passed a castle on the way.
"Let's go inside," said Mr Mould,

"It looks quite picturesque and old."
Teresa saw a sign in red,
"Dungeons to the right," it said.
Unnoticed by the droning guide
She tiptoed from her parents' side,
Along the passage, down the stair,
Through musty chambers dark and bare,
Where spiders hung from chandeliers
Undusted for a hundred years.
"This cupboard's locked!" Teresa cried,
"I wonder what could be inside?"
She picked a hairpin off the floor

And scratched "T. Mould" upon the door.
That instant, with a ghastly din,
The door flew open. From within
A fleshless hand reached out to seize her
And into the cupboard dragged Teresa.
One shriek of terror, sharp and shrill,
The door slammed shut and all was still.

And now it's quite a famous sight
To see the ghostly child in white
Flitting through the gloomy halls
And scribbling on the castle walls.

The Three Billy-Goats-Gruff
Traditional

Once upon a time there were three Billy-Goats who were to go up to the hillside to make themselves fat, and the family name of the three goats was "Gruff."

On the way up was a bridge, over a stream they had to cross; and under the bridge lived a great ugly Troll, with eyes as big as saucers and a nose as long as a poker.

First of all came the youngest Billy-Goat-Gruff to cross the bridge.

"Trip, trap! Trip, trap!" went the bridge.

"WHO'S THAT tripping over my bridge?" roared the Troll.

"Oh! It is only I, the tiniest Billy-Goat-Gruff, and I'm going up the hillside to make myself fat," said the Billy-Goat, with such a small voice.

"Now, I'm coming to gobble you up," said the Troll.

"Oh, no! Please don't take me. I'm too little," said the Billy-Goat. "Wait until the second Billy-Goat-Gruff comes. He's much bigger."

"Well, be off with you!" said the Troll.

A little while after came the second Billy-Goat-Gruff to cross the bridge.

"Trip, trap! Trip, trap!" went the bridge.

"WHO'S THAT tripping over my bridge?" roared the Troll.

"Oh! It's the middle Billy-Goat-Gruff, and I'm going up to the hillside to make myself fat," said the Billy-Goat, who hadn't such a small voice.

"Now, I'm coming to gobble you up," said the Troll.

"Oh, no! Don't take me. Wait a little till the big Billy-Goat-Gruff comes. He's much bigger."

"Very well, be off with you," said the Troll.

But just then came the big Billy-Goat-Gruff.

"*Trip, trap! Trip, trap! Trip, trap!*" went the bridge, for the Billy-Goat-Gruff was so heavy that the bridge creaked and groaned under him.

"WHO'S THAT tramping over my bridge?"
roared the Troll.

"It's I! THE BIG BILLY-GOAT-GRUFF,"
said the Billy-Goat, who had a big hoarse voice
of his own.

"Now, I'm coming to gobble you up," roared
the Troll.

"Well, come along! I've got two spears,
And I'll poke your eyeballs out of your ears.
I've got besides two curling-stones,
And I'll crush you to bits, body and bones."

That was what the big Billy-Goat said. He
flew at the Troll and poked his eyes out with his
horns, and crushed him to bits, body and bones,
and tossed him out into the stream and after that
he went up to the hillside. There the Billy-Goats
got so fat they were scarcely able to walk home
again; and if the fat hasn't fallen off them, why
they're still fat; and so —

Snip, snap, snout,
This tale's told out.

The Dark Wood
Traditional

In the dark, dark wood
Was a dark, dark house,

In the dark, dark house
Was a dark, dark room,

In the dark, dark room
Was a dark, dark cupboard,

In the dark, dark cupboard
Was a dark, dark shelf,

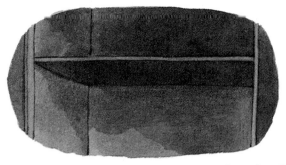

And on the dark, dark shelf
Was a dark, dark box,

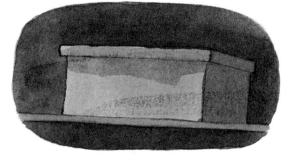

And in that dark, dark box
Was a GHOST!

Elisabeth the Cow Ghost
William Pène du Bois

In a town in Switzerland lived a man named Paul, who had a calf named Elisabeth.

Elisabeth was a cream-colored calf and everybody who saw her would say, "What a gentle calf! What dreamy eyes!"

And when she grew older into a big cream-colored cow, everybody who saw her would say, "Such a gentle cow! And what dreamy eyes!"

And when she grew very old into an aged cream-colored cow, everybody who saw her would say, "What a gentle old cow! And what beautiful dreamy old eyes!"
UNTIL

Elisabeth grew tired of being called so gentle and became quite angry.

After a while she grew awfully old and was ready to die, but just before she died, she heard Paul say, "Isn't it a shame? She is such a gentle cow with such dreamy eyes!"

This made Elisabeth so mad that she decided to come back in the form of a ghost after she died to show everybody how fierce she really was.

She died the next morning and Paul felt awfully sad. He was so sad that he almost forgot his birthday, which was only three days off.

Suddenly Paul had an idea. "I shall have a big

birthday party," said he, "and invite all my friends and have a big celebration."

He hoped this way to forget Elisabeth who made him feel so sad.

That night Paul sat up very late thinking about his party. Suddenly he heard a strange noise in the dining-room. He ran downstairs and found the ghost of a cow floating over the dining-room table.

Then he heard the ghost speak. It said, "I am the ghost of a fierce cow. I shall come and haunt you and scare you every night."

But Paul looked at it carefully and said, "Oh, cow ghost, I can see by your gentle look that you are the ghost of poor Elisabeth, the most gentle cow that ever lived."

At this it was so mad that it floated very fast out of the window, mooing loudly.

The next morning, Paul went to see his friends Yvonne, Jacques and Claude in a nearby village.

He asked them to his party, which was now only two days away. They all said they would come, so he went home and soon it was night.

That night at the same time as the night before he heard a strange noise in the living-room. He ran downstairs and found the ghost of a cow with a big hood over its head and a great spear on its tail.

It was floating over the mantelpiece. It said, "I am the ghost of the fiercest cow that ever existed. I shall haunt you and scare you day and night."

But Paul looked at it carefully and said, "I can see by your cream-colored body that you are the ghost of poor Elisabeth, the most gentle cow I have ever known."

At this it was so angry that it floated with great speed through a crack in the wall and disappeared, mooing and sobbing very sadly.

The next day Paul went to a town which was many miles away. There he saw his friends Pierre, Suzanne and Jeanne and invited them to his party, which was to be the next day. He then returned home, arriving late at night.

When he entered the house he heard strange noises in the kitchen, so he ran in and found the ghost of a cow. It was all covered with sheets, except for little holes for its eyes to see through, and it was floating over the kitchen stove.

Then he heard the ghost speak. It said, "I am the ghost of a cow so fierce that even as a calf I was feared for miles around."

But Paul looked at it with great care and said, "I see by your dreamy eyes that you are the ghost of poor, poor Elisabeth, the most gentle, most kind and playful cow that ever grazed in Switzerland."

At this it snorted, mooed loudly, sobbed sadly and disappeared through a very small hole down the sink.

The next day there was a big party and Yvonne, Claude, Pierre, Jacques, Suzanne and Jeanne all were there.

Everybody had a wonderful time until late at night

WHEN
SUDDENLY

there was a strange noise in the kitchen and then it moved to the living-room, and in the living-room there were grunts, snorts and moo sounds.

Claude was puzzled.
Suzanne was frightened.
Pierre was worried.
Yvonne was curious.
Jacques was startled.
Jeanne was afraid.

But Paul was all these things and also awfully angry because it was his birthday party.

And then an extraordinary-looking ghost entered. It was all covered with sheets, with a hood over its eyes and a spear on its tail, and it snorted very loudly.

It floated over the table and said, "I am the ghost of a cow famous for fierceness and cruelty. I shall haunt and scare you all every moment of your lives."

At this everybody was so scared that they all ran away in all directions, yelling and screaming. They went home feeling very frightened.

Paul was afraid to go home because he was afraid of this terrifying ghost.

He finally walked up to the house and peeked in one window, and then in all the other windows, and seeing no ghost he went in and cautiously went to bed.

He was just going to sleep when he heard a soft mooing downstairs. At this he was furious, so furious that he grabbed a big stick and decided to beat up whatever he met. He ran downstairs, threw open the door, put on the lights, and yelled in his deepest voice, "Who goes there?"

But there before him was floating the ghost of the good cow Elisabeth. Then he heard the ghost speak. It said, "It was I who scared you tonight, Paul. Did I really scare you?"

"Yes," said Paul.

"Did I *really* scare you?" said Elisabeth.

"You certainly did," said Paul.

"Then I am awfully sorry," said Elisabeth, "and I shall never do it again, never never again."

And before Paul could say a thing, it floated out of the window and disappeared into the night.

And this was because Elisabeth was really a very gentle cow with very dreamy eyes.

The Catipoce
James Reeves

"O Harry, Harry! hold me close—
   I fear some animile.
It is the horny Catipoce
   With her outrageous smile!"

Thus spoke the maiden in alarm;
   She had good cause to fear:
The Catipoce can do great harm,
   If any come too near.

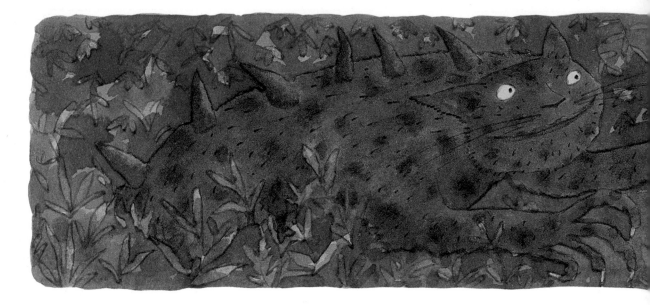

Despite her looks, do not presume
  The creature's ways are mild;
For many have gone mad on whom
  The Catipoce has smiled.

She lurks in woods at close of day
  Among the toadstools soft,
Or sprawls on musty sacks and hay
  In cellar, barn, or loft.

Behind neglected rubbish-dumps
  At dusk your blood will freeze
Only to glimpse her horny humps
  And hear her fatal sneeze.

Run, run! adventurous boy or girl—
   Run home, and do not pause
To feel her breath around you curl,
   And tempt her carrion claws.

Avoid her face: for underneath
   That gentle, fond grimace
Lie four-and-forty crooked teeth—
   My dears, avoid her face!

"O Harry, Harry! hold me close,
   And hold me close a while;
It is the odious Catipoce
   With her devouring smile!"

The Strange Visitor
Joseph Jacobs

A woman was sitting at her reel one night;
  And still she sat, and still she reeled, and still
    she wished for company.

In came a pair of broad broad soles, and sat down
  at the fireside;
  And still she sat, and still she reeled, and still
    she wished for company.

In came a pair of small small legs, and sat down
  on the broad broad soles;
    And still she sat, and still she reeled, and still
      she wished for company.

In came a pair of thick thick knees, and sat down
  on the small small legs;
    And still she sat, and still she reeled, and still
      she wished for company.

In came a pair of thin thin thighs, and sat down
  on the thick thick knees;
    And still she sat, and still she reeled, and still
      she wished for company.

In came a pair of huge huge hips, and sat down
on the thin thin thighs;
And still she sat, and still she reeled, and still
she wished for company.

In came a wee wee waist, and sat down on the
huge huge hips;
And still she sat, and still she reeled, and still
she wished for company.

In came a pair of broad broad shoulders, and sat
down on the wee wee waist;
And still she sat, and still she reeled, and still
she wished for company.

In came a pair of small small arms, and sat down
  on the broad broad shoulders;
    And still she sat, and still she reeled, and still
      she wished for company.

In came a pair of huge huge hands, and sat down
  on the small small arms;
    And still she sat, and still she reeled, and still
      she wished for company.

In came a small small neck, and sat down on the
  broad broad shoulders;
    And still she sat, and still she reeled, and still
      she wished for company.

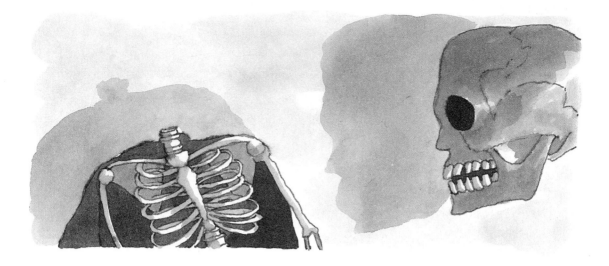

In came a huge huge head, and sat down on the
small small neck.

"How did you get such broad broad feet?" quoth
the woman.
"Much tramping, much tramping" (*gruffly*).

"How did you get such small small legs?"
"Aih-h-h!—late—and wee-e-e—moul" ★
(*whiningly*).

"How did you get such thick thick knees?"
"Much praying, much praying" (*piously*).

★ Up—late—and—little—food.

"How did you get such thin thin thighs?"
"Aih-h-h!—late—and wee-e-e—moul"
  (*whiningly*).

"How did you get such big big hips?"
"Much sitting, much sitting" (*gruffly*).

"How did you get such a wee wee waist?"
"Aih-h-h!—late—and wee-e-e—moul"
  (*whiningly*).

"How did you get such broad broad shoulders?"
"With carrying broom, with carrying broom"
  (*gruffly*).

"How did you get such small small arms?"
"Aih-h-h!—late—and wee-e-e—moul"
  (*whiningly*).

"How did you get such huge huge hands?"
"Threshing with an iron flail, threshing with an
    iron flail" (*gruffly*).

"How did you get such a small small neck?"
"Aih-h-h!—late—and wee-e-e—moul"
    (*pitifully*).

"How did you get such a huge huge head?"
"Much knowledge, much knowledge" (*keenly*).

"What do you come for?"
"FOR YOU!" (*At the top of the voice, with a wave
    of the arm, and a stamp of the feet.*)

Old Roger Is Dead and Laid in His Grave
Traditional

Old Roger is dead and laid in his grave,
  Laid in his grave, laid in his grave;
Old Roger is dead and laid in his grave,
  H'm ha! laid in his grave.

They planted an apple tree over his head,
  Over his head, over his head;
They planted an apple tree over his head,
  H'm ha! over his head.

The apples grew ripe and ready to fall,
   Ready to fall, ready to fall;
The apples grew ripe and ready to fall,
   H'm ha! ready to fall.

There came an old woman a-picking them all,
   A-picking them all, a-picking them all;
There came an old woman a-picking them all,
   H'm ha! picking them all.

Old Roger jumps up and gives her a knock,
   Gives her a knock, gives her a knock;
Which makes the old woman go hipperty-hop,
   H'm ha! hipperty-hop.

The Ghost Who Came out of the Book

Margaret Mahy

There was once a very small ghost who lived in a book—a book of ghost stories, of course. Sometimes people caught a glimpse of it and thought it was some sort of bookmark, but mostly people did not see it at all. When anybody opened the book to read it the ghost slipped out from between the pages and flew around the room, looking at the people and the people's things. Then, when the ghost saw that the person reading the book was growing sleepy or was finishing the story, it slid back into the book and hid between the pages again. There was one page it especially liked with a picture of a haunted house on it.

One evening a child was reading the ghost stories and the ghost slipped out of the book as usual. It flew around the top of the room and looked at spiders' webs in the corners of the ceiling. It tugged at the webs and the spiders came out, thinking they'd caught something. Then the very small ghost shouted "Boo!" at them, frightening them so that they ran back into their cracks and corners to hide. While the ghost was doing this, the child's mother came in, shut the book, kissed the child and put the light out, all in a second or two. The ghost was shut out of the book and left outside in the world of the house.

"Oh, well," said the ghost, quite pleased, "a good chance to try some haunting on a larger scale. I'm getting a bit sick of spiders anyway."

The door was shut with an iron catch so the ghost couldn't get into the rest of the house. It just flew around the bedroom a few times and went to sleep at last in the folds of the curtains, hanging upside-down like a bat.

"What a day to look forward to tomorrow!" it thought happily just before it went to sleep. "I'll scare everyone in the place. I might not bother to go back to the book again."

But alas, the next morning the ghost slept in.

The mother of the house came in briskly and flicked the curtain wide. The ghost, taken by surprise, broke into two or three pieces and had to join up again.

"There's a cobweb up there," the mother of the house said, and before the ghost was properly joined up again she vacuumed it into her vacuum cleaner. Of course, a vacuum cleaner was nothing to a ghost. This ghost just drifted straight out again, but it certainly felt shaken and there was dust all the way through it.

"Now I am getting very angry," the ghost said to itself, and it followed the mother of the house into the kitchen and hissed a small buzzing hiss into her ear.

"Goodness, there's a fly in the kitchen," said the mother, and she took out the fly spray and squirted it in the direction of the hiss.

Being a ghost, the ghost didn't breathe, but the fly spray made it get pins and needles all over and it went zigging and zagging about the kitchen, looking like a piece of cobweb blown about the kitchen by a playful breeze. At last it settled on

the refrigerator.

"I'll just take things quietly for a bit," the ghost whispered to itself. "Things are getting too much for me." It watched the mother dust the window ledges.

"Why does she do that?" the ghost wondered, for the dust looked like speckles of gold and silver and freckles of rainbow. Some dots of dust were like tiny glass wheels with even tinier glass wheels spinning inside them. Some specks were whole worlds with strange islands and mysterious oceans on them, but all too small, too small for anyone but a very small ghost to see.

But when the mother began to make a cake the ghost gasped, for she poured in a measure of sugar that looked like thousands of ice diamonds all spangled and sparkling with white and blue and green. "Let me have a closer look at them," the ghost murmured to itself, and it flew down into the sugar. At that moment the mother of the house began to beat the cake mixture with her electric egg beater.

"Help!" screamed the ghost as it was whirled into the sugar and butter and got runny egg all over it.

The cake mixture was so sticky that the ghost

got rather glued up in it, and before it knew what was happening it was poured into a greased tin and put into the oven. Being a ghost, nothing dangerous could happen to it. In fact the warmth of the oven was soothing and the ghost yawned and decided, as things were so unexpected and alarming outside, to stay where it was. It curled up in the center of the cake and went to sleep.

It did not wake up until tea time. Then it heard voices.

"Oh, boy—cake!" it heard the voices say.

"Yes," said the mother of the house, "I made it this morning." And in the next moment a knife came down and cut the ghost in two. It joined up

again at once, and when the slice was lifted out of the cake the ghost leaped out too, waving in the air like a cobweb and shouting, "Boo!"

"Oh!" cried the children. "A ghost! A ghost! The cake's haunted."

"Nonsense—just a bit of steam," said the mother firmly, touching the cake with the back of her hand. "Funny thing though—it's quite cool."

"Perhaps it's a sort of volcano cake," the father suggested. "Never mind! It tastes lovely."

"It tastes haunted!" the children told each other, for they were clever enough to taste the ghost taste in between the raisins, a little bit sharp and sour like lemon juice.

The ghost meanwhile flew back to the bedroom where the book lived.

"First the whirlwind and then the desert," it said to itself, thinking of the vacuum cleaner and the vacuum cleaner's dust bag. "Then the ray gun and after that the treasure" (thinking of the fly spray and the sunlit dust). "Then the moon-mad-merry-go-round and the warm sleeping place" (that was the electric egg beater and the oven). "And then the sword!" (that was the knife).

"But I did some real haunting at last — oh, yes — real haunting and scared them all. 'Boo!' I cried, and *they* all cried. 'A ghost! A ghost!'"

That night someone picked up the book of ghost stories and opened it at the very page the ghost loved best — the one with a picture of a haunted house on it. The ghost flew in at the door of the haunted house and looked out from behind the curtain of the haunted window. "Home again!" it said. "That's the best place for a small ghost. Small but dangerous," it added. "Quite capable of doing a bit of haunting when it wants to."

Then the book was closed and the very small ghost went to sleep.

The Hairy Toe
Traditional American

Once there was a woman went out to pick beans,
and she found a Hairy Toe.
She took the Hairy Toe home with her,
and that night, when she went to bed,
the wind began to moan and groan.
Away off in the distance
she seemed to hear a voice crying,

"Where's my Hair-r-ry To-o-oe?
Who's got my Hair-r-ry To-o-oe?"

The woman scrooched down,
'way down under the covers,
and about that time
the wind appeared to hit the house,

SMOOSH!

And the old house creaked and cracked
like something was trying to get in.
The voice had come nearer,
almost at the door now,
and it said,

"Where's my Hair-r-ry To-o-oe?
Who's got my Hair-r-ry To-o-oe?"

The woman scrooched further down
under the covers
and pulled them tight around her head.
The wind growled around the house
like some big animal
and r-r-umbled
over the chimney.
All at once she heard the door cr-r-a-ack
and Something slipped in
and began to creep over the floor.
The floor went
cre-e-eak, cre-e-eak
at every step that thing took toward her bed.
The woman could almost feel
it bending over her head.

Then in an awful voice it said:

"Where's my Hair-r-ry To-o-oe?
Who's got my Hair-r-ry To-o-oe?

YOU'VE GOT IT!"

The Small Ghostie
Barbara Ireson

When it's late and it's dark
And everyone sleeps . . . *shhh shhh shhh,*
Into our kitchen
A small ghostie creeps . . . *shhh shhh shhh,*

We hear knocking and raps
And then rattles and taps,

Then he clatters and clangs
And he batters and bangs,

And he whistles and yowls
And he screeches and howls . . .

So we pull up our covers over our heads
And we block up our ears and WE STAY IN
OUR BEDS!

Jackie and the Ogre
James Reeves

"JACKIE," called his mother one day, "will you get the broom and sweep the stairs for me?"

Jackie did as he was asked, and in a corner he found a sixpence. As he put it in his pocket, he said to himself:

"Now, what shall I buy with it? Shall I buy some dates? I am very fond of dates."

Then he remembered that if he bought dates, he would have to throw away the stones, and that would be a waste.

"No," he said, "better to buy a bag of nuts. But then I should have to throw away the shells. I'll buy some figs. With figs there is nothing to throw away."

So Jackie bought himself some figs and climbed up his favorite tree to eat them. When he had nearly finished, an ogre saw him and called out from below:

"Hullo, Jackie, what have you got there?"

"Figs," said Jackie with his mouth full.

"I'd like one of them," said the ogre. "Hand me one down."

Jackie did as he was asked, and instantly the ogre seized his hand and pulled him out of the tree. Then he opened his sack and pushed Jackie in. It was not figs he wanted but Jackie, who he thought would make a tasty stew. He quickly tied up the sack, threw it over his back and strode home, roaring out at the top of his voice:

"Wife, wife! I've caught Jackie. We will have him stewed for dinner. Make up the fire and boil some water."

When he got home, the ogre put down the sack on the ground and went indoors to see that his wife was getting the pot ready for the stew.

"You must go into the garden," she said, "and get me some vegetables. I shall need onions, carrots, a turnip and some fresh herbs."

The ogre went into the garden to do as he was told. While he was doing this, Jackie took out his pocket knife and cut a hole in the side of the sack. He jumped out, put three big stones into the sack and ran for his life. Then the ogre came out for the sack. As soon as he found that Jackie had

escaped, leaving nothing but three big stones, he bellowed with anger and told his wife there would be no stewed boy that day; they would have to make do with a rabbit. He swore to be revenged on Jackie.

Next day the ogre went everywhere in search of the boy. He strode all round the town, up streets and alleys and all round the market place. Then suddenly he heard Jackie laughing at him.

"Hullo, ogre!" called Jackie, who was sitting astride a roof, high above a horse-pond. "Did you enjoy your stew? I hope it tasted good."

"You are a very clever boy," said the ogre. "How did you get up on that roof?"

"Oh, that was easy," answered Jackie. "I made a great pile of dishes and plates and glasses and pans and kettles, and on this I climbed up to the roof. Why don't you come up beside me?"

The ogre decided to climb up in the same way, so that he could get hold of Jackie once more and pay him back for escaping. So he made a great pile of dishes and plates and all the other things Jackie had spoken of. Then he began to climb. When he was near the top, there was a tremendous crash of broken crockery, and the ogre toppled over and fell headlong. He landed in the horse-pond, and there was a splash which could be heard all over the town. How Jackie laughed, and how all the people shouted and clapped their hands.

Jackie ran home and told his mother what had happened. His mother gave him a slice of cake big enough to stop him laughing for a good five minutes.

Two Witches' Charms
Ben Jonson

The weather is fair, the wind is good:
Up, dame, on your horse of wood!
Or else tuck up your gray frock,
And saddle your goat or your green cock,
And make his bridle a ball of thread
To toll up how many miles you have rid.
Quickly come away,
For we all stay.

The owl is abroad, the bat and the toad,
    And so is the cat-a-mountain;
The ant and the mole sit both in a hole,
    And the frog peeps out of the fountain.
The dogs they do bay, and the timbrels play,
    The spindle is now a-turning;
The moon it is red, and the stars are fled,
    But the sky is a-burning.

The Little Wee Tyke
Traditional

There was a little wee tyke and he wasn't so big as the house-cat, so nobody wanted him. They said he was no use at all and they were going to drown him when a poor, ragged little lassie begged for him and got him.

She ran home with him, "Mammy! I've brought a little wee tyke!" she cried.

"There's no water for the porridge," said her mother. "The well's bewitched. He'll die of thirst like us all."

"Not if I'm about," said the little wee tyke. "Let me alone to deal with this."

Then the farmer came in.

"I can't get out to my sheep," he said. "The gate's bewitched and the ewes and lambs need watching against hill foxes."

"Not if I'm about," said the little wee tyke. "Leave me alone to deal with them."

Then the son came in.

"The cow's bewitched. There's not a drop of milk to sell."

Then his little boy came in.

"The hens are bewitched. There's no eggs and they'll never cackle or walk about any more."

"Not if I'm about," said the little wee tyke. "Let me alone to deal with this."

"You!" they all cried out angrily. "Get out!" They started to throw things at him. The little lassie picked him up. "You!" said the little lassie. "Could you? Would you?"

"I would and what's more I will," said the little wee tyke and out the door he went.

"He can't get out any more than we can," said the farmer. But he had.

"You can't pass through," said the gate. "Old Witch Nanny laid it on me to keep back all who belong here."

"I don't belong here *yet*," said the little wee tyke and he went through to the sheep. After he rounded them up so nicely and quietly into the fold by the wall he went back to the hen-house and carried the twelve hens safe inside. "I don't belong here *yet* so I'll break the mischief on you. When I've fetched your water, you can each lay an egg for me."

Then he went down to the well and the family were all watching by now. He scratched all round where the spring ran out. "Old Witch

Nanny laid it on me not to run freely for any who belong here," said the well. "I don't belong here *yet*," said the little wee tyke and he kicked away the witchstone and the water ran all down by the door and the mother got a pailful for the porridge.

Then the farmer went out to the fold and the little boy ran and found twelve eggs, and the cow was milked.

"You all said we needed a dog," said the little lassie.

"I've not done yet," said the little wee tyke.

But they all came running back and crying, "The witch is on her way here!" and ran to bolt the door, but the little wee tyke said, "Let me out first. I'll deal with her," and they shut him out and the little lassie cried.

Old Witch Nanny walked widdershins all round the farm. "That'll hold them fast," she cackled.

"Oh no, it won't. Not a bit," barked the little wee tyke, "because I've come behind you backward and scratched your footprints all out."

Old Witch Nanny turned around in terror and

dropped her broom. "That's clever, that is," said the little wee tyke, and stood *across* it and then all she dare do was shriek "Scat!" at him.

"I'm not a house-cat," said the little wee tyke. "I can use my teeth as well as bark."

Then Old Nanny the witch tried to climb up

the roof but the little wee tyke took a good bite of her left leg and hung on as she climbed. When he let go she fell off the roof and lay in the farmyard. "I'm dying!" she whimpered.

"Not just yet," said the little wee tyke. "Old Nick has got to fetch you and we don't want him here — and he don't like the look of me and my teeth. Take yourself away and die Somewhere Else before he takes you there!"

And away she hobbled and crawled right out of sight. And there was thunder and lightning and a great green flame.

Then the little lassie called the little wee tyke to come in.

"I don't belong," said the little wee tyke.

"We all want you," said the little boy.

"I'm too small," said the little wee tyke.

"You got good teeth," said the father.

"You won't chase me with the poker or throw things at me, or tread on me when I'm sleeping?"

"Never!" they cried, and the little lassie brought him a bowl of milk.

And when he had lapped it all up he came in. "This is about my size," he said, and went to sleep in one of the farmer's slippers.